JUV/E
ND
553
.M7
L4
1995

WALKER

Chicago Public Library

W9-BCR-854

A blue butterfly : a story about Cl

7/06
2

Walker Branch
11071 South Hoyne
Chicago, IL 60643

A Blue Butterfly

A STORY ABOUT Claude Monet

BIJOU LE TORD ~ A Doubleday Book for Young Readers

For Carol,
with love.

The author wishes to express her
warmest thanks to Mme Nelly W. Wallays
of the Foundation Claude Monet in Giverny,
for allowing her the freedom to go about, take
photographs and paint at will in Monet's garden.

A Doubleday Book for Young Readers
Published by
Delacorte Press
Bantam Doubleday Dell Publishing Group, Inc.
1540 Broadway
New York, New York 10036
Doubleday and the portrayal of an anchor with a dolphin are
trademarks of Bantam Doubleday Dell Publishing Group, Inc.

Copyright © 1995 by Bijou Le Tord
All rights reserved. No part of this book may be reproduced or
transmitted in any form or by any means, electronic or mechanical,
including photocopying, recording, or by any information storage
and retrieval system, without the written permission of the Publisher,
except where permitted by law.

Library of Congress Cataloging-in-Publication Data
Le Tord, Bijou.
A blue butterfly : a story about Claude Monet / by Bijou Le Tord.
p. cm.
ISBN 0-385-31102-8
1. Monet, Claude, 1840-1926~Themes, motives~Juvenile literature.
[1. Monet, Claude, 1840-1926. 2. Artists. 3. Art appreciation.]
I. Title.
ND553.M7L4 1995
759.4-dc20   94-38779
                                                 CIP
                                                 AC
The text of this book is set in 14 point Colwell Handletter.
Book design by Trish Parcell Watts
Printed in U.S.A.
September 1995
10 9 8 7

Author's Note

During the short trip I made to Paris and Giverny in preparing for this book, I was extremely lucky to see more of Claude Monet's paintings than most people are privileged to see in a lifetime.

If Monet could have watched me looking intently at each of his paintings, he probably would have smiled. And perhaps he was there—I think he was—when I first walked in his garden in Giverny, amazed at the multicolored flowers and the beautiful and forever changing light of the French countryside. Somehow, nothing I had seen or felt until then prepared me for what I was about to encounter at the Musée de L'Orangerie in Paris. This museum was built to house Monet's now world-famous *Water Lilies* paintings. As I stood there gaping at the pair of astonishing paintings, I had to humbly ask myself: How did he do it, using so few colors?

When I was ready to paint my Monet book, I hoped I would have the courage to use the same colors Monet used. And I did, following a list he had worked with in the latter part of his life. We now know that the list was incomplete. It shows only eight colors: silver white, cobalt violet light, emerald green, ultramarine extra-fine, vermilion (*rarely*), cadmium yellow light, cadmium yellow dark, and lemon yellow. "*And that's all!*" as Monet himself exclaimed.

It was not easy for me to use someone else's palette. But by some strange coincidence, as I was to find out many times in the course of this project, my own colors were very close to those of Monet. At times I added the burnt sienna and cobalt blue Monet used earlier in his life. On my own I used Payne's gray as a substitute for black, which I found almost impossible to do without. Payne's gray is a dark gray blue. I do hope I have done justice to Monsieur Monet's colors.

Here is a partial list of museums in the United States and France where you can see Claude Monet's paintings:

United States—NEW YORK: Brooklyn Museum; Metropolitan Museum of Art; Museum of Modern Art. BOSTON: Museum of Fine Arts. CAMBRIDGE: Fogg Art Museum. CHICAGO: Art Institute of Chicago. CLEVELAND: Cleveland Museum of Art. LOS ANGELES: Los Angeles County Museum of Art. PHILADELPHIA: Philadelphia Museum of Art. PITTSBURGH: Carnegie Museum of Art. SAN FRANCISCO: California Palace of the Legion of Honor. WASHINGTON, D.C.: National Gallery of Art.

France—HONFLEUR: Musée Eugène Boudin. LE HAVRE: Nouveau Musée des Beaux Arts-André Malraux. LYON: Musée des Beaux-Arts. PARIS: Musée Marmottan (here you also can see some of Monet's private objects, such as his glasses, paintbrushes and palette); Musée de L'Orangerie; Musée D'Orsay. GIVERNY: Although the Musée Claude Monet in Giverny has no original Monet paintings, this is where Monet lived. You can visit his house and the garden where he painted. You'll want to walk over the Japanese bridge he built and, in summer, look at the water lilies in bloom. There is also a replica of his "Norvégienne" boat.

Walker Branch
11071 South Hoyne
Chicago, IL 60643

In
his
garden
in
Giverny,

Claude Monet
painted

flowers,

like
tiny
jewels

or
little
stars,

leaping
from
the
sky.

He
sometimes
painted
them

set
in
a field
of
wheat

or
oats,

with
rich
colors

of
vermilion,

emerald,

apricot
and
violet.

They
were
poppies

fluttering

in
the
wind,

tulips,
irises

and
water
lilies,
unfolding

their
secrets
to
the
light.

Monet
never
thought
that
anything
was
impossible.

He
painted
in

the
cold
of
winter,

in
ice and
snow,

in
fine
rain

and in
wild
wind.

He
painted

in
his
studio

boat,

or
standing

high
on
a cliff,

facing

the
turbulent
sea.

He
painted
furiously

from
dawn

to
twilight,

to
pin
down

the
sun

and the
clouds,

and
place
them

lovingly

in
his
paintings.

Monet

painted
as
a
bird
sings,

for
himself.

He
could
see
things

in
a
way

no one
else
could.

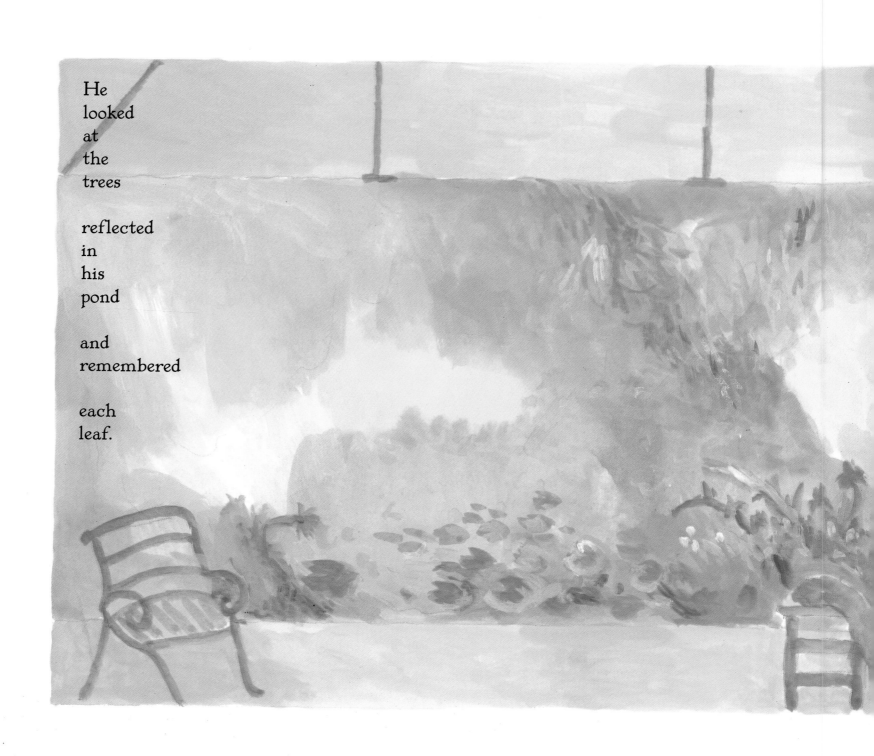

He
looked
at
the
trees

reflected
in
his
pond

and
remembered

each
leaf.

He
painted,

dazzled

by
the
light

he
held

on
his
brush,

just
for

an
instant,

like
a
blue

butterfly.